Flintstone has disappeared! When he reappears (policeman in tow) he's minus his bag. And we're only at Euston station, and the Great London Soccer Weekend hasn't even started.

Up and down escalators. More bags nicked. Missed connections. Frayed nerves. And when we get to play match number one we're greeted by a geezer with Santa Claus whiskers and a striped rugby-club tie.

Rugby! Compromise: soccer first half, rugby next half. We flatten the sweat-bands and scrum-caps 6-1 and scarper.

But the big news is Chippy. Is he about to be shot down in flames?

PS. Cock-ups courtesy of Harry Hennessy, last seen disappearing at Crewe station in search of a strong cup of tea

Peter Regan

RIVERSIDE
The London Trip

Illustrated by Terry Myler

THE CHILDREN'S PRESS

To

Connor and Hayley Dennis

First published 1998 by
The Children's Press
an imprint of Anvil Books
45 Palmerston Road, Dublin 6

2 4 6 5 3

© Text Peter Regan 1998
© Illustrations The Children's Press

ISBN 1 901737 16 0

All characters are fictional.
Any resemblance to real persons, living or dead,
is purely coincidental.

Typeset by Computertype Limited
Printed by Colour Books Limited

Contents

1 'Big-head' Chippy

Hello, it's me, Jimmy Quinn.

Five weeks time it's April, meaning me and the gang will be going on a football trip to London with Riverside Boys. We were to fly, but not now. We're going by ship and rail instead, and all because Mr Glynn, our football manager, says Harry Hennessy is too fat to fit in an aeroplane seat.

Last month we had a meeting in Harry Hennessy's house (he helps with the team) to think of ways to fund our trip to London. Most of us can make money, no bother, but we weren't going to tell Harry Hennessy; he'd only spend the proceeds on Guinness. So we said nothing, that's except Flintstone McKay. And he only opened his mouth because he's as thick as two planks.

'We'll get our mammies to bake a cake.'

'Wha' ye mean, Flintstone?'

'He means nothin'. Nothin' at all. He

doesn't know what he's talkin' about.'

'I do. Some Sundays there's cake sales in the Holy Redeemer after Mass. The priest announces it off the altar. They all go into the parish hall afterwards an' buy cakes. We'd make a fortune.'

'To have a cake sale we'd have to be from there. None of us are from that parish.'

'How would the priest know?' asked Chippy O'Brien, our star player. 'We can go to Mass there a few Sundays.'

'How'll that make it all right?'

'Well, if we all go to Mass together, an' sit up the front, he's bound to notice us, especially when Mad Victor gets goin'. He's great at prayers. Even those down the back would hear him. When the priest gets to know us, he'll let us have the parish hall.'

'You can count me right out,' said Harry Hennessy. 'I'm goin' to no Holy Redeemer. I'm a Protestant.'

We all knew Harry wasn't a Protestant. He was confused. He didn't know what he was.

Anyway, we agreed to have a cake sale,

once we got use of the parish hall. The idea was to get all our mothers to bake cakes and scones. Chippy even suggested we go to all the bakeries in Bray last thing on Saturday evening and ask for anything that was left over.

'Think they'd do that?'

'Course they would. There's always somethin' left over. They'd be gone off by Monday. They make Chester cakes with some and throw the rest out.'

'I want no leftovers.'

'It wouldn't be for us. Whoever bought wouldn't know, not unless you told them. You wouldn't tell them, would you?'

'No.'

For one, Mad Victor didn't like the idea of the cake sale. At least, not the sale part.

'I don't think we should sell the cakes. It would be a waste.'

'Wha' ye mean, Victor?'

'We should eat them instead. Have a cake feast. It'd be great.'

'Don't be daft. The idea of the cake sale is to

make money, not make pigs of ourselves. Money is what matters, not a fancy cake with pineapple and cream on it.'

And money would matter.

The cake feast was a non-starter.

The cake sale was very definitely up and running.

On the football scene, we weren't doing too well in the Dublin Schoolboys League. But we were going really well in the Dublin Cup. With Chippy being on the Dublin Schoolboys panel (and almost a certainty to be on the Irish Schoolboys team), it really inspired the rest of us to play above ourselves in the Dublin Cup.

We'd already won a few cup matches and were due to play Wayside Celtic for a place in the quarter-final. We felt we could beat them, especially as we were the home team, and nobody ever beats us in Bray Park. We are invincible there. Once Belvedere beat us 7-nil away, but we stuffed them in the return match. Even better, Mad Victor gave them wrong directions going home and they ended up in

Wicklow instead of Dublin.

We were due to play the cup game against Wayside Celtic in a week's time, a few weeks before our trip to London. We were finding it hard to think about the match. All we were interested in was the cake sale and the upcoming trip to England.

There were other things on our minds too. Chippy, on the verge of becoming a schoolboy international, was getting big-headed. He didn't want to be seen shoving the wheelbarrow we used for selling vegetables. He didn't want to knock on doors either, trying to sell the stuff. Lately, he was dressing real neat and didn't want to get his clothes dirty. He didn't mind taking the money though, once Flintstone and me finished the round on Friday and Saturday nights.

Neither was there any point in complaining, as we relied on Chippy to buy all the fruit-'n'-veg off his uncle. He wouldn't deal with us, only Chippy. We hadn't any choice, except to soldier on and give Chippy as little as possible. That's if we could outsmart him.

There wasn't much chance of that happening.

It all came to a head one Friday night in the middle of Beech Road.

'We're cuttin' ye out, Chippy. You won't do any work. All you do is take the money.'

'Ye can't expect me to work. You don't see Ryan Giggs pushin' a barrow. He's to think of his image.'

'Ye're not Ryan Giggs, Chippy.'

'I might be someday.'

'It's not fair, us doin' all the work, an' you gettin' half the profit.'

'I supply all the fruit-'n'-veg, don't I? I'm entitled to somethin'.'

'We'll give you commission instead.'

'What kind of commission?'

'Five per cent of the profits.'

'That'd only be about two quid.'

'It's enough, especially when ye do nothin' except dowse yerself in perfume.'

'It's not perfume. It's after-shave.'

Chippy was shaving! None of the rest of us, except Sonny Clarke, shaved. We were afraid, in case we'd cut ourselves and end up covered in elastoplast. We'd too many pimples on our faces. We'd rather grow beards than shave, at least until we were done with pimples. There was an epidemic of pimples around our way. Everybody had them. At least everybody who was over fourteen-and-a-half, and played football.

It ended up we had to give Chippy fifteen per cent of our profits. It was hardly worth our while but we decided to struggle on, at least until the trip to London came up. We intended to review the situation afterwards, maybe cut Chippy out altogether, buy our own fruit-'n'-veg elsewhere.

But we hadn't reckoned on Chippy. When the time came he got his own back. But that's for another day – another scam.

2 Into the Quarter-finals

Mr Glynn and Harry Hennessy got permission from the parish priest of the Holy Redeemer to hold a cake sale. Seemingly the parish priest remembered us all sitting up at the front of the church at Mass the previous Sunday.

He remembered Harry Hennessy too.

But not from Mass, but from wobbling around the streets at night.

Still, whatever about Harry, we got the parish hall for the cake sale. We would have to make a small donation towards the church and leave the hall spick and span afterwards. Other than that there were no further strings attached. The name of the hall was the Little Flower Hall.

We had all asked our mothers to bake cakes. Mad Victor's mother was especially pleased. She had only recently come back from England after being missing for years. When Mad Victor asked her to bake some cakes she cried. There must have been something about cakes that made her cry. She baked about three dozen and got Princess to give her a hand.

Princess is Mad Victor's half-sister. She is almost five, but a real angel. She comes to most of our matches along with her dad, Terry O'Sullivan, who is from Jamaica. That makes him dark, and Princess kind of dark. It also makes him Victor and Henry's stepfather.

They live in a big house in a posh part of Bray. There's a garden half the size of Bray sea front. That means Mad Victor and his little brother, Mad Henry, have their own football pitch to play on, and plenty of trees to swing from.

Victor and Henry just love to swing from trees. Once Victor held a tree-swinging competition and he had us entered for it. Victor won, no bother, and Princess presented him with a silver salver she'd taken from her mother's sideboard.

We explored the house after that. Victor's ma and da had gone out, so we investigated the place, every cupboard, even the attic.

Growler Hughes took a shower and locked himself into the conservatory in the hope that he'd get a suntan like most professional footballers have, especially Italian footballers.

Growler never got a suntan. But we found out later that Victor's ma had a sun-bed and he asked us over to the house whenever she was out, so we all got to use the sun-bed. Flintstone got tanned so bad he looked more like Princess than one of us, the main difference being he is two feet taller than her.

By the time the cup game against Wayside Celtic was played we all had suntans, only some of us got bleached hair and we didn't look too good. But we didn't let the look of our hair get us down. We were good and ready for Wayside and beat them 2-nil, putting us through to the quarter-final.

Mr Glynn got straight on the phone to the fixtures secretary.

'Make sure you don't give us a fixture for the first weekend in April.'

'Why, what's on the first weekend in April?'

'Our trip to London.'

'You should have mentioned it before now.'
'I did, two weeks ago.'
'You should have put it in writing.'
'You never said so.'
'Well, I'm saying so now.'
'I'll do it first thing in the morning.'
'You've left it a bit late.'
'What do you mean?'
'Like I said, you've left it late.'
'Do your best.'
Just then, the phone went dead.
He'd do his best all right, his best against us.

He wasn't called Little Hitler for nothing. What's more, there was nothing little about him. He was overgrown. If he was any bigger he'd block out the sun. Everyone who plays soccer calls him Little Hitler.

Chippy was in the habit of calling him that when he was away playing football for the Dublin Schoolboys League – Chippy is good at name-calling, especially if he doesn't like someone. Maybe that was why Little Hitler wouldn't do us any favours in future regarding soccer fixtures.

Chippy was getting on like a house on fire with the Dublin Schoolboys U-15 team. Not only that, but he'd played a few trial matches for the Irish Schoolboys team. He didn't tell us much about what was going on, but we knew he was doing all right.

Sometimes he'd come home with loads of training gear. Once he had two Mitre footballs and a spray for numbing sprains, just like what professional trainers use when treating players on the side of the pitch in the English Premiership. Most of us bought bits of training gear off him. We got it for half nothing.

He tried to sell the two Mitre footballs to Mr Glynn. But Mr Glynn wouldn't buy them.

'They're nicked,' he said.

'They're not!' lied Chippy. 'I found them in a ditch.'

He'd found them in a ditch all right, only they'd been kicked there accidentally on purpose by Chippy. Whoever was in charge of training was too lazy to fish them out. Chippy brought them home afterwards.

Mr Glynn wouldn't have anything to do with the two Mitre footballs. But that didn't mean Harry Hennessy wasn't interested.

'I'll take them,' he volunteered.

We were surprised Chippy handed them over free of charge. He must have gone momentarily brain-dead, probably from spraying his hair with the sprain spray.

That was the last we saw of the Mitre footballs. Harry Hennessy probably sold them and put the proceeds into the fund he had for buying Guinness. Not that there was much in the fund. It was always on flow – into the pocket of the owner of Harry's favourite pub. The man drives a big flash car, and owns a big fancy house. We sometimes call the house 'the house that Harry built', and the car 'the car that Harry bought'.

When it comes to school we're not over-smart. But when it comes to money we're dead bright!

3 Chippy Throws a Punch

The day of the cake sale duly arrived. Mr Glynn had set up a committee to make sure enough cakes were baked and to collect the Saturday leftovers from the bakeries and supermarkets in Bray. None of us were allowed on the committee. We weren't even allowed to help on the day as the cake sale clashed with a match we had against Pearse Rovers from Sallynoggin. Mr Glynn got Harry Hennessy to take us to the match.

What's more, we had to do without Mr Glynn's minibus. It was needed to collect the cakes and have them good and ready for eleven o'clock in the Little Flower Hall.

On the Sunday, we met early at the bottom of Bray Main Street. The bus, the 45A, wasn't due for another half an hour. Mad Victor had Henry and Princess in tow.

Harry Hennessy was in great form. While we were waiting he gave us a quick run-down on Pearse Rovers' history. Harry is really sentimental. Sometimes teardrops form in his eyes when he thinks about the past.

'Years ago Pearse Rovers were the Number One club in Sallynoggin.'

'That so, Harry?'

'Yeah, until St Joseph's came on the scene.'

'When was that, Harry? A hundred years ago?'

'No, about forty. Things changed after that. A Father McCabe came on the scene. He had a Volkswagen Beetle.'

'What's a Volkswagen Beetle, Harry?'

'A make of car. He used it to put the players in an' bring them to the matches.'

'That's what Mr Glynn did with Riverside before we got the minibus.'

'Yeah, just like George Glynn used to do. Only George Glynn ain't Father McCabe.'

'Wha' ye mean, Harry?'

'Well, priests can get things done that ordinary people wouldn't have an earthly of. People listened to Father McCabe. They opened doors for him.'

'They close them for us,' moaned Growler Hughes.

'Yeah, and that's wha' happened to Pearse Rovers. St Joseph's took over.'

'Think we could get Father Bourke on our committee, Harry? Maybe a few doors would open then.'

'Not an earthly. Father Bourke has enough to do runnin' around Little Bray without lookin' after the likes of us.'

Just in case you don't know, Father Bourke is the parish priest of Little Bray – our parish.

Around about then the bus came. Once the driver saw who was standing at the bus stop he totally ignored us and drove on.

'Never mind,' said Harry, 'there's another bus in half an hour.'

'Not on a Sunday, there isn't,' reminded Chippy. 'There's none for an hour.'

'We'll try an' thumb a lift.'

And that's what we did.

Three of the lads got a lift, no bother.

Then another three.

Then the milkman came along. He took

eight, including Princess.

That left Harry Hennessy and Mad Henry. The plan was if they didn't get a lift they'd wait for the next bus. In the end, Mad Henry went home in a sulk as Harry Hennessy wouldn't give him a loan of the bus fare.

At the pitch, we tried to hold out for Harry Hennessy to arrive to pick the team and fill in the referee's card. But the referee couldn't wait all day, so Chippy did the necessary.

Growler Hughes went ape when Chippy didn't pick him. Growler was always on the team. After Chippy he's our best player. He must have done Chippy a bad turn. But whatever it was Chippy wouldn't tell us. So Growler was only a sub. Without him on the team we hadn't a proper centre-half. Our defence would be paper thin.

We weren't long in finding out. Within five minutes we were a goal down. Mad Victor pulled a goal back but then gave away a penalty.

Then Growler and Chippy began to row with one another. Pearse scored another goal.

Still no sign of Harry Hennessy.

Growler came out on the pitch and told Flintstone to get off, that he was taking over. The referee had to halt the game until it was all sorted out.

It ended up with Chippy walking off the pitch in protest over Growler coming on.

Then Harry Hennessy arrived ....

If Mr Glynn had been present instead of being back in Bray looking after the cake sale, none of it would have happened, and we probably would have walloped Pearse Rovers. As it was we got beaten 5-2.

That wasn't the end of our woes.

Some skinhead who was watching the match passed a comment about Princess's colour. Chippy heard him and chased him along the sideline until he caught up with him and a few punches were thrown.

The referee was over like a flash, and as Chippy was still wearing football gear he took his name and said he was reporting him to the League. But that didn't stop Chippy throwing a few more punches and cursing the referee

from a height.

Harry Hennessy was clueless; he didn't know what to do. He just stood there, watched it all happen.

We knew that Chippy would be in big trouble with the League; we couldn't see him walking free. He'd get suspended, Dublin Schoolboys star or not. We'd probably end up losing a good few more matches before the season would be over.

When we got back to Bray most of us made a beeline for the Little Flower Hall. We knew

Mr Glynn would still be there tidying up. We were mad keen to see how the cake sale went.

Business must have been good. There wasn't a cake to be seen, only torn pieces of cardboard platters and raffle tickets. All the cakes were gone except for some crumbs that were being swept into black refuse sacks.

There were a few oul' ones, including my two sisters Fiona and Kathleen, giving Mr Glynn a hand.

We didn't stay long, just long enough to try and find out how much money was made on the cake sale.

But Mr Glynn wouldn't tell us, said he hadn't time to count it yet.

There were a few other things he didn't tell us either. Like the two posh neighbours' kids he took on the rounds with him when he collected the leftovers from the supermarkets on the Saturday night.

'He didn't want us because we're rough lookin',' whispered Flintstone.

'Wha' ye mean?'

'Go home an' look at yerself in a mirror.'

'Why should I do tha'?'

'You'll see wha' I mean. Our clothes are kinda shabby, an' all that.'

'Speak for yerself,' said Mad Victor. 'There's nothin' shabby about me. I'm always wearin' brand-new gear. Wha' I'm wearin' now me ma just got from the shops yesterday.'

Sadly, the rest of us couldn't say the same, as Christmas and the January sales only came once a year. In bad weather we looked like farmers, dressed like them and all.

One other thing happened at the cake sale which, unfortunately for me, everybody else knew about.

My da arrived just before the raffle wearing an extra long long-sleeved overcoat. First prize was a giant-sized box of chocolates. The tickets were cloakroom tickets. When the time came for the draw my da dipped his hand into the cardboard box the tickets were in and drew his own ticket – only the ticket had been up his sleeve all the time. That didn't stop him from getting the box of chocolates. He devoured them.

Once I heard that I got out of the hall as quick as I could.

We didn't bother telling Mr Glynn about what happened to Chippy at the match. We left it to Harry Hennessy. Either that, or he could wait until the League sent a letter requesting Chippy to appear before the disciplinary committee.

What surprised us after the match was that Harry Hennessy didn't go to the pub. Instead he brought Princess home just in case she was down in the dumps over the skinhead calling her names. It showed Harry Hennessy was considerate. What's more, he didn't bother giving out to Chippy for chasing the skinhead around the pitch. Harry probably would have done the same too, only he wasn't up to it. The skinhead had nothing to do with Pearse Rovers. He just happened to be there.

Rough luck in a way that Chippy was the property of the League.

In the eyes of the League Chippy, not the skinhead, would have to shoulder the blame.

4 Filling in the Details

The day after the cake sale Mr Glynn told us to ask our parents if they'd like to come on the trip to London. He said four would be nice.

'Why should we bring parents, Mr Glynn?'

'Because we need a few extra adults to give a hand. It's a big responsibility. Two adults would find it very hard to manage on their own. The extra help would be appreciated.'

The extra help might have been appreciated by Mr Glynn, but not by us. We were fed up looking at our parents every day of the week. None of us wanted them along, except for Mad Victor, and he was only interested because he'd just got his ma back lately and parents were kind of new to him.

So, bar Victor, none of the lads mentioned Mr Glynn's request to any of their parents. I wouldn't have either, only for Chippy. He was still sulking over his drop in income from the vegetable round, so to get his own back he mentioned the trip to my ma and da.

'Like to go on the trip to London, Mr Quinn?'

'How much is it?'

'About a hundred and fifty quid.'

'I wouldn't have that kind of money. A hundred and fifty smackers!'

And he wasn't telling lies. There's no way my da can hold on to money. Soon as he sees sight of the stuff he's down to the bookies to lose it on a horse.

Chippy then asked my ma.

'Like to go on the trip to London, Mrs Quinn?'

'I'd love to, only…'

'Only what?'

'I have to look after Jimmy's da.'

Ma wasn't joking. My da has to be looked after. He's useless. One of the few things he's good at is juggling the dinner-plates when he's doing the washing-up. Only problem; he smashes a few off the ceiling.

Once it became obvious that no parents, apart from Terry O'Sullivan, Mad Victor's stepfather, would be making the trip, we cheered up no end. See, we don't regard Terry O'Sullivan as a real parent. Well, not insofar as Mad Victor and Henry are concerned. So we didn't mind him coming on the trip.

Anyway, we were getting to like him. He had Victor and Henry dressed in the best of clothes, meaning they didn't look half as rough as they used to. He had bought Victor a cam-recorder. Mad Victor was putting it to good use. He said he was going to make a film some day. All the neighbours would be in it. He said he'd film them unawares; through gaps in hedgerows, through downstairs windows, that kind of carry-on. The film would be great, especially since most of the people around our way are nuts.

He was going to consider me to write the script. Why? Because I write stories when I'm in the humour. I'm the youngest writer in Ireland, though I haven't been published as yet. Not unless you'd call a few bits of graffiti on street walls being published.

No, Terry O'Sullivan was very good to

Victor and Henry, so we wouldn't mind in the least if he came on the trip to London, especially if he'd be as good to us as he was to Mad Victor and Henry.

So far we knew very few details of the trip to London. We knew how much we had to pay, how long we were going for, what time we were to meet at. But being as curious as cats we wanted to know more, so we had plenty of questions to ask Mr Glynn.

'Where in London are we goin' to, Mr Glynn?'

'Islington.'

'Where are we stayin', Mr Glynn?'

'In a hotel.'

'Are we playin' any matches?'

'Two. Gavin Byrne arranged one, Harry Hennessy the other.'

Once we heard Gavin Byrne's name mentioned we were over the moon. We are all great fans of Gavin Byrne. And why not? He's an Irish international who plays for one of the top teams in the English Premiership. Their pitch is near Islington and we'd probably get to see him play while we were over there. Maybe meet some of the team.

'How did you get in touch with Gavin Byrne, Mr Glynn? Was it through Lar Homes?'

'No, we wrote to Gavin in England and he wrote back. He's arranged everything.'

We should have known Mr Glynn wouldn't get in touch with Lar Holmes. They didn't get on, mainly because of football. Lar Holmes ran Shamrock Boys from Greystones, the schoolboy club Gavin Byrne had played for.

None of us had much contact with Shamrock Boys as they hadn't a team at our age group as such. We played them twice in six years in mess matches. But we were in the habit of calling Lar Holmes names any time we'd see him in Bray. All the older Riverside players called him names so we thought it best to carry on the tradition, because that's what all football clubs are about – tradition. But if Gavin Byrne looked after us well in London we'd probably give up calling Lar Holmes names as a kind of favour.

'My cousin used to play for Riverside against Gavin Byrne,' said Flintstone, just after Mr Glynn told us about Gavin Byrne.

'Who's your cousin, Flintstone?'

'Chopper Doyle.'

'Chopper Doyle?'

'Yeah, Chopper Doyle.'

We all idolized Chopper. He is the biggest hero Riverside ever produced. He's on the telly every second week, only he doesn't play football any more. He's a jockey. He sends lots of tips to Harry Hennessy. They all win. Sometimes Harry tells us, other times he won't. Says we shouldn't be going into betting shops, that we'll only grow up to be idlers.

If my da knew Harry Hennessy was getting winning tips off Chopper he'd invite him over to live in the house full-time.

So would we all. We could do with some extra money for the trip to London.

Like the saying goes: 'No money, no fun.'

My two sisters dropped a bombshell the other day.

'We're movin' out, Da.'

'Wha' ye mean?'

'We're movin' into a flat.'

'A flat! How're ye goin' to pay for it? You're not even workin'.'

'We are. We started two months ago.'

'How come no one ever told me? How come ye never tell me anythin'?'

'We did, Da. You weren't listenin'.'

'Did ye tell yer ma?'

'Of course. She doesn't mind.'

I didn't mind either. Imagine, getting rid of

my sisters. Maybe I'd get to put a dart-board and a snooker table in their room. Rid of them after a lifetime! I'd thought I'd never see the day.

'Ye're too young to leave home. You's are only fifteen.'

'Da, we are eighteen and nineteen.'

'Still too young. I won't allow it.'

Maybe Da wouldn't allow it, but his say didn't matter, not any more. Not as far as my sisters were concerned. In a few weeks' time they'd just pack their bags and go. I'd even pack them for them, but I knew they wouldn't let me. At worst I'd carry the bags to wherever the flat was and keep my fingers crossed they'd never come back. Da, he was heart-broken. He'd have no one to read the paper to him, and only Ma to make him a cup of tea. He was facing hard times, real hardship.

I wrote a bit of a poem when I heard my sisters were moving out.

Want to hear it?

No?

Well, you're going to hear it anyway:

Sisters
  Grow up
    And leave
      Home.

Brothers,
  They stay
    And become
      Men.

Sisters
  Go,
    And brothers
      Stay.

Then
  Da dies;
    Ma
      Cries.

Sisters
  Leave,
    And brothers
      Inherit.

There was no way I was going to show the poem to Ma or Da. But I'd consider sending it to my sisters' new address when I'd be sending Christmas cards again. Among other things, I'd be letting them know I had a brain, that I'm not a male chauven...male pig, or whatever the word is that women always shout at men, especially fat women.

But it just shows you, where there's property going it's always the male who gets it. That's why my sisters were getting out early. They were making a head-start.

Not that we own the house we live in. We only have it rented off the Council. But we might someday; that's if Da overcomes his addiction to gambling and wins the Lotto all in the one go.

My sisters leaving home came as a real surprise. It was pure good news.

I only hoped bad news wouldn't be long in following. Like they'd be back home again a few weeks later.

5 Lourdes Celtic

We were expecting word from the League regarding Chippy being called before the disciplinary committee. But Mr Glynn said it would take a few weeks before anything would happen. Instead, we had the upcoming match at the weekend to look forward to. It was to be the long-awaited Dublin Cup quarter-final against Lourdes Celtic.

The night before Mr Glynn had the entire team around to his house for a team talk.

'This match,' he said, 'is the most important you've ever played. Win this and you're in the semi-final of the Dublin Cup.'

But Flintstone wasn't having any of it. 'We've played important matches before, Mr Glynn. We've been in cup finals before. We nearly won the League twice.'

'But that wasn't in Dublin, it was in Wicklow. Dublin's the big one. You've never been this far before.'

Thinking back on it, we'd never been beyond the second round before.

'See this here,' continued Mr Glynn. He had taken a blackboard from behind a door. 'There are a few tactical moves I want to go through. Dead-ball situations.'

'It's no use doin' them on a blackboard, Mr Glynn. We'd rather do them for real. Blackboards only muddle us.'

What Flintstone said was the truth – blackboards confused us. To understand, you only had to see the agony we all go through in school once a blackboard is used. We are all hopeless as far as blackboards go. Even Chippy, crafty and all that he is.

We couldn't get the hang of what Mr Glynn was going on about. There he was, pointing out who was to move this way, that way, and every other way, and leave a channel for Chippy to cannon the ball into the net.

It didn't take long for Flintstone to start complaining again.

'Mr Glynn, I've a ball. It'd be better if we went outside and practised the free-kicks.'

Mr Glynn agreed, so we all piled outside on to the front lawn, near enough to a street light.

There was a bit of a drizzle. Nobody wanted to place their coats on the damp ground. But Flintstone didn't mind. He put his coat down for one post, and his jumper for the other. Flintstone is a great club man. He wins the Clubman of the Year award every year. He'd do anything for Riverside Boys, even play in his bare feet if he had to.

We tried Mr Glynn's ideas for free-kicks a few times, but once the lads in the defensive wall got to know what was going on the free-kicks weren't worth a curse.

Mr Glynn called for a change of plan; a different kind of free-kick. Only the ball went off course and straight through the sitting-room window. Suffice to say the window wasn't open. But it might as well have been once the ball smashed through the glass.

There was a row over what happened. But we didn't get any of the blame. Mr Glynn got it all. His wife tore him out of it.

'Just practising a move,' he mumbled.

'Well then, we'll all practise a move,' she retorted, and smacked him straight across the face with a tea-towel.

We didn't wait to see any more. We trooped out of the front gate and said we'd meet him first thing in the morning.

We knew Mr Glynn would be in for a hard night.

Us, we didn't care, we just marched off. Whatever about Mr Glynn and the broken window we'd be good and ready for the Dublin Cup game the next day.

No matter what, we were always good and ready. Like Chippy says, 'We're that good and ready we should be in the Boy Scouts.'

The Dublin Cup game against Lourdes Celtic was an eleven o'clock kick-off. The pitch was covered in mud. It was hard to see the markings, especially the penalty areas.

'The areas ain't marked, ref,' moaned Chippy. He had a point. It was important to him. Because once Chippy got into the area he was lethal; there was only one way to stop him, and that was to bring him down.

'Ye can't even see the penalty spot,' fumed Harry Hennessy.

'Doesn't matter,' said the ref. 'I ref here every week. I know exactly where everything is.'

'Did ye hear wha' he said?'

'Yeah. He's dopey. How could he know when there's no markings?'

We all knew the rules, that's except for Flintstone and Mad Victor. We knew the pitch should be properly marked out. Failing that the match shouldn't be played – it should have been called off by the referee.

'Hey, ref,' shouted Harry Hennessy, 'come over here a minute.' Being an ex-referee he knew all about rules and regulations. He wanted a word with the ref, just to let him know we weren't complete eejits.

But the ref didn't want to know, told us to get togged out so as he could get the game started.

He said, 'All Cup games have to be played this weekend, regardless.'

'Who says so?'

'The fixtures secretary. There's a backlog of matches.'

The fixtures secretary was the chap Chippy calls Little Hitler. The man on the League committee that Mr Glynn was in touch with about our trip to England.

Well, if the fixtures secretary said the game had to be played that was that. Rules or no rules we'd have to get out on the pitch and play. We could row about it afterwards. Maybe protest to the League if we lost. The other team viewed the situation likewise.

Before we went out on the pitch we checked the showers in case we'd need a wash afterwards. There was only a dribble. Though there was a gush of water from the taps on the wash-hand-basins. At least we would get the muck off our faces before going home.

As for the match, it was a shambles. It ended up a scoreless draw.

Soon as the final whistle went we made straight for the wash-hand-basins. Arms, legs faces, necks – the lot got a good wash. It wasn't easy getting our feet in, but we managed. We left the place in a right mess.

Lourdes Celtic weren't too happy with the draw. They knew we'd give them a right walloping in Bray.

We were due to go on the trip to London the following Friday and we wouldn't be back until early Monday morning. The Dubs Cup replay would probably be on the following Sunday. That suited us fine.

It suited Mr Glynn and Harry Hennessy too. It suited us all.

6 Littler Hitler

Next day Mr Glynn received a letter from the Dublin Schoolboys League. When Mr Glynn mentioned it to us we thought it was a complaint concerning Chippy chasing the skinhead around Pearse Rovers' pitch. But it wasn't; it was something else.

'What's it about, Mr Glynn?'

'About? It's a damned disgrace! They're saying we have to play the cup replay against Lourdes Celtic next Sunday.'

'That means we can't go on the trip?'

'Not likely. I'll be on the phone right away to Little Hitler. Two months ago he said it was okay to go on the trip to London. I even got permission to play two friendlies. He said he'd leave that weekend free. I should have got it in writing, instead of over the phone. If I had, there would be no problem now.'

But there was a problem.

Mr Glynn got on the phone straight away.

'Hello, it's me, George Glynn, Riverside Boys.'

'What can I do for you?'

'Do? By the look of things, nothing. Listen, you gave us permission to go on a trip to London this coming weekend.'

'So what?'

'I got a letter this morning, saying we have to play a cup replay next weekend.'

'You should have notified me about the weekend in writing.'

'Not originally I didn't. But I did two weeks ago. You told me to do it.'

'I got no letter. Anyway, it wouldn't make any difference.'

'How not?'

'Cup games take precedence.'

'Only over League fixtures. You said you'd leave us free next weekend.'

'How was I to know your cup game would go to a replay? There's already a serious backlog. The replay has to be next weekend. Either that, or give a walk-over.'

'Give a walk-over?'

'Yes. There's no way the fixture can be called off. It has to be got out of the way.'

'But, that's not fair. There must be some other way out of it.'

'Cancel the trip to London.'

'No way.'

'Well, then it looks like a walk-over for Lourdes Celtic. Enjoy your trip to London.'

'Don't worry, we will.'

Mr Glynn hung up and told us the bad news. He said it was too late to call off the trip to London so we'd have to give a walk-over.

'Could we not get other lads to play in our place, Mr Glynn?'

'No way, there would be trouble. We have to play ourselves. Either that or give a walk-over.'

'Give the walk-over, Mr Glynn.'

'Yeah, give the walk-over.'

We were all mad keen to see London, going on a ship and all that.

The cup would have to wait for another year.

We'd heard of Hitler dropping a few bombs in his day.

Now, Little Hitler was following suit.

We wouldn't forget in a hurry.

Next night, Tuesday night, some of us organised a raffle during the interval of a cabaret all the women around our way go to. It's always on the first Tuesday of the month; Children's Allowance Day. Only problem was we knew Mrs O'Leary, our favourite 'oul' wan', would be there. But we kept well away from her. We weren't allowed in anyway. We hung around the door just to see how the raffle would go, and to collect the proceeds from the management.

We'd told the manager the money would be for the trip to London and that we'd be handing it over to Mr Glynn. But we were telling lies. The money wouldn't be handed over to Mr Glynn; we'd be keeping it for ourselves as pocket-money. Neither Mr Glynn nor Harry Hennessy knew anything about the raffle, and we weren't going to tell them.

First prize in the raffle was a canary and cage Mad Victor got from a birdman in Palermo. Well, he got the canary from the birdman. The cage was one he found in a skip.

We knew the bird and cage would go down a treat because everybody up our way is mad into birds. If you were to ask most of them what their favourite film is they'd tell you *Birdman of Alcatraz.* In appreciation, Ray Parker (Robert Browning), our local poet, wrote a poem, 'Faith of our Feathers,' and stuffed it through their letter-boxes. We just couldn't go wrong raffling a canary and cage.

On the night, Chippy showed up with a fish. It was a mullet he got out of the harbour. It didn't look too good. It looked that bad we knew no one would buy it.

'Nobody'd want that. Bring it home an' give it to the cat.'

'No way, it's too good a money-earner to do that. It's not goin' to no hungry cat. It's too valuable.'

'Ye must be jokin'.'

'I was down in Mayo once, in a place called

Ballina. It's a great place for salmon. They had this kinda fair with all different stalls. This lad had a stall with a salmon he was makin' money on.'

'Ye're forgettin' one thing, Chippy. That's no salmon, it's a mullet. You'd have to pay people to take it away. It's bleedin' horrible.'

'Ye're missin' the point. I won't be *sellin'* the mullet. I'll use it to make money, have a "Guess-the-Weight" competition. We can harge fifty pence a go an' give the winner thirty quid.'

'Sayin' if we don't make thirty quid?'

'Don't worry, they'll be mad on it. We'll make a fortune.'

And Chippy was proven to be correct. We made £100 on the Guess-the-Weight competition and £80 on the canary and cage draw. What's more the owner of the cabaret threw in a £50 donation.

Mrs O'Leary won nothing. But she got to keep the mullet. Chippy pinned it to her hat just before the cabaret ended. Being tipsy, she didn't notice the difference and wore it home.

She probably ate it for her supper.

At least, we hoped she did.

Thursday morning Mr Glynn got another letter in the post from Little Hitler. He wouldn't tell us what it contained.

'It'll do until after the trip to London.'

'Tell us now, Mr Glynn.'

'Is it to do with Chippy, Mr Glynn?'

'Maybe.'

Mr Glynn didn't have to say any more; we knew it concerned Chippy. Probably Little

Hitler making a mountain out of a molehill.

Thursday afternoon, Terry O'Sullivan pulled out of the trip. Princess too. He said she mightn't feel up to it, especially without him. We could see the logic, but only up to a point. Princess had plenty of family in London; all aunts and uncles who were either born in London or Jamaica.

We all wanted Princess on the trip, but we got Mad Henry instead.

Mr Glynn and Harry Hennessy weren't too happy about it.

'Why can't you come?' they said to Terry.

'I've to look after the business. It's only newly established, man. Can't go runnin' off, not so soon.'

'But we need the help.'

'So do we all, man.'

'Sixteen kids to look after, plus Henry. We'll never manage.'

'Maybe it ain't cricket, but you'll get by.'

'It's all right for you. You can walk away from it. We can't.'

'Easy. I got a warehouse full of problems. I don't walk away. I stay, do the job.'

'Give us a break.'

'Nothin' to do with me. The trip is yours. You thought it up. It's your baby, man.'

'We never thought it would get this far. At least, we thought we'd get some help from parents. We'll never be able to keep an eye on them, not on our own.'

'Well, that's the way it is, man. Face up an' get on with the job. Me, I'm off to work.'

Mr Glynn and Harry Hennessy watched Terry O'Sullivan drive off to Sandyford Industrial Estate in his flash BMW. He had a warehouse full of merchandise to unload on Dublin's Pound Shops. It was time to get started.

Mr Glynn and Harry Hennessy didn't have anything to unload, except us. And unlike Terry O'Sullivan, they had no last-minute excuse and had to take us on the trip.

Well, they'd hardly let us go on our own.

7 On the Boat

We were all up early on the morning of Friday, the 4th. Flintstone was up at half-four. He had two cats and four dogs to feed, as well as double-checking to make sure he left nothing behind.

Yes, Friday the 4th was the date of our long-awaited trip to London. Our only regret was giving Lourdes Celtic a walk-over in the Cup. The tie was to be played on Sunday morning, but we'd be in Battersea Park, London, then, playing a game against a team Gavin Byrne organised.

We were due to meet at seven at the bottom of the estate. Mr Glynn and Harry Hennessy had booked a coach to take us to Dun Laoghaire for the ferry. Some of our parents came down the road to see us off, but not too many. I think they were glad to see us going. Maybe, they were hoping we wouldn't come back. At least, I knew that's the way my da and two sisters felt.

'Wha's the name of the ship ye're goin' on?'

'Don't know, Da? Why, does it matter?'

'No, not really. Only, I was hopin' it would be the *Titanic*.'

Ma was horrified. 'Jimmy, don't be sayin' things like that.'

'Think I meant it? It's only a joke, Mary.'

'Well, don't say it again.'

'I won't.'

Me, I didn't care what Da said – or my sisters. I was really surprised when he gave me a fiver towards the trip. It was the first time I got anything off him since I made my Holy Communion. Though, that's not quite true; he gave me a tenner when I made my Confirmation. He asked for it back the next day. It was a good job we were on our way to England, and pronto. He'd have a long way to travel to get the fiver back.

Terry O'Sullivan, and Princess showed up at the coach to see us off. Mad Henry was also there; Terry O'Sullivan said he could act as the team mascot, especially on account of having two friendly matches in London.

Terry O'Sullivan took a few photos before we got on the coach. Mad Henry, on account of being the team mascot, got in the photo-call as well. He was dressed as a leprechaun, all in green. He looked like something out of *Darby O'Gill and the Little People*. We thought it a bit daft, but Mad Henry thought it real cool. You only had to look at him to see he was as proud as Punch.

Before the coach left five of us ran down the road and made four different abusive phone-calls to Little Hitler. Somehow Chippy had come across his home phone number when off playing with the Dublin Schoolboys. We made the phone-calls because we wanted to be sure Little Hitler would make a bad start to the day. We would have made a fifth call, only Little Hitler gave up answering the phone, and we weren't going to hang on listening to the engaged tone. In any case we had other things on our mind right then.

We ran back to the coach just in case it left without us. Deep down we knew it wouldn't,

but we were that hyped over the trip we weren't able to think straight. None of us had been to England, never been on a ship. We could hardly wait. We were out of our minds with excitement. If a stranger came along he'd have a job figuring out which of us was Mad Victor. We were that hyped it was hard to tell the difference.

Mr Glynn could see the difference though. He kept telling us to calm down, but we passed no heed.

The coach driver wasn't over happy when

he saw us. 'I thought this trip was for the girls' club,' he said to Mr Glynn.

'What do you mean?'

'Well, it was a woman who booked the coach.'

'That was my wife.'

'She said it was Riverside girls' team.'

'We haven't got a girls' team. You must have misunderstood her.'

'She definitely said a girls' team. If I knew it was this lot I wouldn't have bothered comin'.'

But he had come and that was what mattered. Mad Henry had brought a catapult. He sat next to a window. But as the window wasn't a proper window he couldn't open it. The idea was to load up the catapult with an arsenal of overripe tomatoes and let them loose on the early morning traffic. But on account of not being able to open the window he gave up on the idea, saved the tomatoes for the sea journey, and got talking to me about an idea he had for a football story.

'Where did ye get the idea from?' I asked him.

'Just thought it up. You bein' into writin' I thought I'd tell ye. It's all about this fella playin' football. He's got a pair of magic football boots. When he puts them on he's deadly, the best player goin'. He can do anythin' with a ball when he's wearin' them, scores great goals, deadly, everythin' the best players in the world can do. Only, when he becomes great he loses the boots. In the end, he finds one of the boots an' becomes more than half-deadly again.'

'How come?'

'It's the right boot. An' he's right-footed. It makes him at least half-deadly.'

'That's daft.'

'Wha' ye mean?'

'Why can't he find both boots an' be done with it?'

'I never thought of that. Ye could have a magic football in the story too. It would make it more interestin'.'

'What age are you, Henry?'

'Ten. Why?'

'I was just wonderin'.'

'Good idea, isn't it?'

'Wha'?'

'The magic football boots.'

'Suppose it is.'

Henry was big into magic. That was one of the reasons he dressed up as a leprechaun for the trip. He thought, maybe, there'd be a crock of gold somewhere down the line. If he found it he'd share it with all the little lads who live around our way. They'd have feasts and sweets for the rest of their lives, that's until their teeth fell out. But that wouldn't be for years to come, and Henry never thought of years down the road; he only thought of today, tomorrow and the day after.

The coach-driver wasn't long in getting us to the ferry terminal in Dun Laoghaire. The sooner he was rid of us the better. Though we were all well-behaved enough. Apart from the phone-calls to Little Hitler it was too early to mess.

'When do you want me back?' he asked Mr Glynn.

'Half-six Monday morning.'

'Be good and ready. I'm not waitin' for them to come off the boat in dribs and drabs. Another thing, they needn't bring half the ship with them. This is a coach, not a juggernaut. Too much over the top and it won't get on this coach. It can stay put on the footpath.'

'Mister, we only got two hands.'

'Yeah, one for your gear an' the other for what you pick up on the way home.'

We didn't bother answering him. We just got off and into the terminal building as quick as we could. But the coach-driver was partly correct. Most of us had spare bags for the return trip. All our parents had given us extra money to load up with duty-free cigarettes and spirits – if we could get it.

Our parents smoke like troopers. Growler's ma smokes that much smoke comes out her mouth every time she speaks.

'Look, she's on fire.'

'Naw, she's only havin' a smoke.'

'I don't see no cigarette.'

'She hid it. She doesn't want ye to see her smokin' in case she'd set a bad example.'

Our parents are real good at telling us what not to do. Only, we are even better; we just go out and do it.

Within minutes we were on the ship, running up and down between decks, shouting to one another what was on offer.

We left it to Mr Glynn and Harry Hennessy to sort out somewhere to sit. Us, we were gone. Mad Henry got as far as the car-deck. He began pestering the drivers, asking if they wanted their windscreens washed. The drivers didn't know what to make of him, dressed in his leprechaun outfit. Some Yanks took photographs of him sitting on the bonnet of a car. He charged £1 a go, and got £6 before he was grabbed by a member of the crew and brought back to Mr Glynn and Harry Hennessy. But within five minutes he was off again, this time to launch his arsenal of tomatoes (from a safe distance) at some oul' wans he thought might be related to Mrs O'Leary.

8 Miracle of the Chips

Once the ship got clear of the harbour we went off with Harry Hennessy on a tour. The first place he headed for was the duty-free, but it wasn't open. Not until the ship got outside the 12-mile limit. But we found a gambling saloon of sorts with slot-machines and roulette. We liked the roulette best because the fellow operating it was wearing a dinner-jacket. We thought he looked real cool. He wouldn't let us play, so we got Harry Hennessy to play for us. We all crowded around and slipped him a few bob to put on. Mad Henry sat up front, because we felt he'd bring luck.

Unusually, Chippy didn't take much interest. Normally, he'd be in the thick of the action, but not this time. He sat down on his own. I went over to him.

'What's wrong, Chippy?'

'Nothin' much.'

'Seasick?'

'Naw. I was thinkin' those phone-calls we made to Little Hitler could get me into trouble. He'll know who it was.'

'So wha'? He can't touch us.'

'Maybe not, but he could get at me.'

'How?'

'He could get me thrown off the Dublin Schoolboys team. Ask the Irish Schoolboys not to consider me.'

'They'd never drop you, Chippy. Ye're too good.'

'Don't know. It happens, especially with the Irish Schoolboys. They don't want messers on their teams. I've been in trouble already for bits of messin'. The spot of bother with the skinhead won't help either.'

'They'll do nothin'.'

'That's what's got me worried. They will.'

I'd never seen Chippy so badly upset. It wasn't like him. He was always the life and soul of everything. I'd never seen him like this before, sitting around moping. Maybe there was more going on behind the scenes with the Dublin Schoolboys than he was telling us.

Maybe things were going badly for Chippy, only we didn't know it.

I went back to the roulette but said nothing to the other lads about Chippy. I figured he'd cheer up in time.

We didn't last long at the roulette-wheel. The management cleared us out, so we roamed around for the rest of the trip.

It didn't take the ferry long to get to Holyhead. We were a little disappointed with that. We were only getting used to the sea-trip part of the journey when it was all over.

We didn't think much of Holyhead, that's not until Nigger Doyle told us his uncle had a chip-shop down the road from the harbour.

'He's dead nice,' Nigger told us. 'He always sends money for me birthday. Said if I'm ever over in Holyhead to go to his chip-shop an' he'll give me a feed of chips.'

'That so?'

'Yeah, he'd give us all chips. Why don't we go down an' get some chips off him?'

'He'd hardly be open this early in the morning.'

'We'll knock him up. He won't mind.'

We were to get the London train just across from where the ship docked, but it wasn't due to pull out for another hour.

Mr Glynn had seats pre-booked on it. We were very impressed to see stickers on the seats saying: RESERVED – RIVERSIDE BOYS; it made us feel very important, like we were some top team on tour. We got our bags on to the train as fast as we could told Mr Glynn and Harry Hennessy we were going to the toilets, and beat it off as fast as we could to Nigger's uncle's, all seventeen of us, Chippy included.

Nigger's uncle got some surprise when he saw seventeen lads standing on the footpath outside his chipper. At first he told us to go away. But when he recognised Nigger, and saw Mad Henry in the leprechaun outfit, his heart softened, and tears came into his eyes. In the end, he welcomed us in. I reckoned if we were to do a reel and play some ceilé music he'd have given us the whole shop for nothing.

As it was we all got a bag of chips, two sausages and a burger each. In a way it was like that miracle when Jesus fed the loaves and fish to the crowds. Only difference was, we were the crowd and Nigger's uncle was Jesus.

9 Underground

By the time we got back to the train we were rightly full to the brim.

'Where were you?'

'We were gettin' fed by Jesus.'

'Don't be swearin'.'

'I'm not swearin'.

What d'you mean, "by Jesus"?'

Just then the train pulled out, leaving behind Holyhead, the land of chips, sausages, burgers… and miracles.

Nothing much happened on the train that hadn't already happened on the ferry. Only difference, Chippy had cheered up a lot and won all before him at the poker school we'd set up. We didn't mind, because most of what he won wasn't our money. It belonged to a few oul' lads we got talking to from somewhere down the West of Ireland. They thought they were poker sharks, but they knew the difference once we got dug in.

The only other people we got to know real well were the ticket-collector, a fellow with a tea-trolley, and some grumpy oul' lad in a uniform who acted like he owned the train and we'd no right to be on it. Mad Victor said he was the train guard, but he wasn't. He was an army colonel gone off his rocker. He thought he was on his way to Iraq to kidnap Saddam Hussein and bring him back to England. He took a shine to some of us too. He tried to arrest Growler Hughes, only Growler escaped and hid in the next carriage.

When we saw London we nearly died of fright. There were buildings and streets everywhere. We were expecting the train to halt any second but it kept on going past miles and miles of more streets and buildings. In the end we thought it would never stop, that maybe London stretched all the way to where the sea connects to France. But at last it did halt and we were smack, bang, wallop in the middle of a station with EUSTON plastered all over it.

The place was teeming with people going

home from work. Here we were in Euston railway station, London, not knowing how to get to wherever it was we were supposed to go. We hadn't as much as a map or a compass. Mr Glynn only had a scrap of paper with the address of the hotel in Islington, wherever that was supposed to be.

'Excuse me, how do we get to this address?' he asked someone.

There was a slight problem; the person Mr Glynn asked didn't speak English.

The second person only spoke Japanese.

The third just spoke a few words of English. He kept on saying he was from St Et-tea-n, wherever that was. We got fed up with him saying the one thing over and over, so we asked an old lady who was passing by.

She told us how to get there. We'd have to get the Tube, change at such and such a station, and the place was only a few hundred yards away. We'd find it, no bother, she said. 'In fact,' she added, 'you can't miss it.'

Normally we wouldn't have minded, but with all our football gear and bits of luggage, and the rush-hour crowd milling about us in a right heave-ho, it wasn't easy going.

We made for the connecting Underground station, via Euston. Harry Hennessy led the way. On account of being so fat he was easy to pick out in the crowd, so he made a good leader. That and the fact that he said he'd been in London before.

'He can be like Davy Crockett,' chirped Flintstone.

'Why Davy Crockett?'

'Because Davy Crockett was a scout on the old American frontier. Harry can be like him and show us the way.'

Unlike Davy Crockett, Harry Hennessy didn't have a fur hat. Neither did he know the territory like Davy Crockett did in the Old West. Also he hadn't been in London since he was two. He was as clueless as the rest of us.

'Where's the Underground, Mister?' we asked this definitely English-looking fella with a brief-case and bowler-hat.

'Follow me,' he said in a posh accent.

We followed him, all nineteen of us. But we

lost him in the crowd, so we followed the crowd instead. We had to wait to get into a lift. That split us up, as we couldn't all get in together. So we got in in dribs and drabs, and waited to regroup at the far end.

'Mr Glynn, Flintstone's missin'.'

So he was. Mr Glynn and Harry Hennessy guided us into a corner, out of the rush, and told us to wait until they went back up in the lift to see if they could find Flintstone. They found him all right. There was a policeman with him.

'Mr Glynn, someone stole me bag.'

'The one with your football gear in it?'

'Naw, the one with me pyjamas an' spare clothes. I'll have nothin' to sleep in. I'll have to wear what's on me.'

'You can wear your football gear.'

Seemingly, Flintstone left the bag on the ground for a few seconds. When he went to pick it up it was gone.

'Maybe one of those men with a bowler-hat took it by mistake, thinking it was their brief-case.'

'Mr Glynn, if that was so there'd be a brief-case in its place. No, Mr Glynn, it's been nicked. No one with a bowler-hat took it. It was one of those fellas with a turban.'

There were a good few fellows with turbans mixed in with the crowd. We'd never seen lads with turbans before, except in the pictures.

The policeman handed Flintstone back to Mr Glynn. But Flintstone wanted to go off into the crowd and get his pyjamas back. Instead, Mr Glynn shoved him into the lift. In no time at all he was back with the rest of us.

From there, we had to go down a few escalators.

'Mr Glynn, me bag's gone too. Only it's me football gear.'

And it was. This time it was Nigger Doyle.

'Mine's gone too!'

'And mine.'

That was a total loss of some clothes, a pair of pyjamas and three sets of football gear.

'Hold on to everythin'. Leave nothin' down,' fumed Harry Hennessy, pure red in the face and beady with sweat, as if he'd just met a furnace head-on.

'But we have to leave them down, Harry. We're nackered.'

Eventually, we got to the Underground. There was a map on the wall. It showed all the different places the trains went. There were that many places and so many different lines, we could hardly find where we wanted to go.

Seconds later there was a swoosh of noise as a narrow train thundered out of the darkness into the light of the platform. We weren't sure whether it was our train or not.

'Is it ours, Mr Glynn?'

'Let me check the map and find out.'

Ten seconds later Growler Hughes tipped Mr Glynn on the shoulder. 'Ye'd wanna check quicker, the train's gone.'

Most of the people were also gone. A minute later the platform was full again. It was almost as if the place hadn't emptied at all.

'Gawd, Mr Glynn, wha'll happen if the lights go out?'

'They won't.'

'They could, ye know. Lights always go out, sometime.'

'They have a back-up service.'

'You sure?'

'Course I'm sure.'

Then Mad Victor started. 'Hurry up, Mr Glynn, sort the map out. I'm nervous down here. The whole place could cave-in.'

Soon as Victor opened his mouth we were all nervous as hell. There we were, hundreds of feet below ground, trains roaring through the tunnel almost as quick as we could blink. What with the vibration, the place could collapse any minute.

'It won't cave-in. The Underground's been built over a hundred years, and nothing's ever caved-in.'

'A hundred years! Mr Glynn, that's ancient. Let's get outa here an' get a bus.'

But Mr Glynn didn't want to know. He kept looking at the map, trying to figure the best way to get to Islington. It was more complicated than it looked, because we'd have to change trains. That's if we could figure the correct train to get on in the first place.

Finally, Mr Glynn made a decision. 'This is our train, let's go.'

It wasn't so much a question of going; we were more carried by the push of the crowd on to the train. We were squashed in like sardines. It was worse for the oul' lad standing in front of Harry Hennessy. He had Harry's oversized belly to contend with.

He began to complain. Said Harry shouldn't be allowed on the Tube during rush-hour, that he was taking up too much room.

'I paid me fare…full fare,' retorted Harry.

'I'm entitled to get on whenever I like.'

'You Irish?' asked the man.

'You English?' snapped Harry.

We knew Harry's temper was rising.

So too did the oul' lad. He turned his back on Harry and looked the other way.

Suddenly there was a shout.

'All out…all out!'

'Why, Mr Glynn?'

'Because this is the change for Islington.'

'You sure, Mr Glynn?'

'Course I'm sure.'

When we got off I discovered I'd left my football gear on the train. No way was I going to get it back. The train was well gone, half way to Shepherd Bush for all I knew.

With the amount of football gear that had gone missing you'd think we'd be worried about what was going to happen to the two matches due to be played. But we weren't. We're all football crazy. We'd play in our underpants and vests if we had to, all in white, a new kind of Leeds United effort.

10 Arrival!

An hour later, we were still changing trains. Only good thing was the crowds had thinned out and we were able to get seats.

'Never thought London was this big,' said Flintstone, wiping the sweat from his brow. 'Imagine, two hours on the Underground, an' we still haven't seen daylight.'

'That's because we're lost,' retorted Growler Hughes. 'Another hour an' we'll end up in Australia. We're lost, ain't we, Mr Glynn?'

'Not really. Just a few wrong changes, that's all.'

'I'm starvin', Mr Glynn.' This time it was Mad Victor. 'When do we get somethin' to eat?'

'Soon as we get to the digs.'

'By the way we're goin', that'll be never. Can't we stay with the Salvation Army? Me uncles always stay with the Salvation Army when they're in London.'

'That's only for down-and-outs. We're not down-and-outs.'

'If we're down here much longer whizzin' around every ten minutes on a different train, it won't be long before we're down-an'-outs. We'll never see daylight again!'

Most of us were inclined to believe Victor, mad and all that he was. We'd spent so much time underground we'd begun to think we were Snow White's dwarfs especially when we looked at Mad Henry in his green leprechaun outfit.

Harry Hennessy tried to cheer us up. 'Not to worry,' he said. 'With the crowd dyin' down we'll find our way easy enough. It was just bad timin' to arrive in London durin' the rush-hour, that's all. Now that there's a bit of peace we'll find our way, no bother. It'll all be forgotten about, soon as we get to the digs. Anyway, I've a special treat on for tomorrow.'

'What's that, Harry?'

'Ye'll be goin' on a tour of Wembley Stadium. It'll be great. Do ye a world of good. Me mates played in Wembley once. Only a few Bray people got to do that.'

'Wha' team did they play for, Harry?'

'None. Me mates were workin' there on a buildin' job. They played on the pitch durin' their lunch-break.'

Twenty minutes later, we made the right connection. After that, we found the digs, no bother. We felt right eejits. No wonder the old lady we met on the Underground said we couldn't miss it. It was that big, even if we were blind, we would have walked straight into it.

Gavin Byrne wasn't there though. We felt disappointed about that. He was away in Newcastle for a Premiership game the next day (Saturday) at St James's Park. He left a letter at the reception desk addressed to Mr Glynn, detailing the arrangements he'd made for us: the friendly game and a tour around his club's ground, both on Sunday. He said if he got back from Newcastle on time he'd meet up with us on the Sunday, probably at the match he'd arranged for us in Battersea Park.

The digs weren't digs as such; more a

luxury hotel. After what happened on the Underground we expected something to go wrong, like there wouldn't be enough beds and we'd have to sleep on the floor. But we ended up in the lap of luxury. The hotel was that great we felt like staying put and not going out at all. That way nothing else could go wrong and we'd be safe.

But our curiosity got the better of us.

Soon as Mr Glynn turned his back we were gone.

But we didn't get very far.

The police brought us back.

11 A Confession

Soon as Mr Glynn had sorted things out with the police he made us all go to bed, except for Chippy. He allowed him to stay up and watch TV.

Then Harry Hennessy chipped in: 'Goin' out for a few pints. See ye in the mornin'.'

'Mind you don't get lost, Harry.'

'Get lost? Never! I know where I'm goin'.'

'How could you? You haven't been in London since you were two. It took you all your time to find this place.'

'Maybe I was a bit fuzzy at first. But, it's all comin' back now. Anyway, I never forget a pub.'

Who wouldn't believe him? When it comes to pubs Harry is a genius. Like Chippy once said, 'Ever hear of a bloodhound? Well, Harry's like one, only he's a pubhound.'

So Harry Hennessy went off to the pub and Mr Glynn and Chippy watched telly. The rest of us were packed off to bed. I had to share a room with Nigger Doyle. He didn't have to count sheep to sleep; I did. I couldn't sleep. I was probably overtired. I got up, got out a pen and paper, thought I'd try and write a poem to pass the time. I'd never written outside Ireland.

The idea appealed to me. The poem would form the start of my English collection. I'd get a stamp in the morning. That way I'd have the Queen's head looking down on the completed poem. You couldn't get any more English than

that. I wrote the poem on a scrap of paper. Then I tidied it up and transferred it to a hotel menu I'd taken from the dining-room, though I had to squeeze some of the words in around the various dishes. When I finished I autographed it; that way it would be more valuable in years to come.

For some,
    Lost
        Is a place
            That
                Can't be found.

For others,
    It
        Is a dangerous
            State
                Of Mind.

Lost and Found:
    Two
        Twin opposites
            That
                Can't be one.

Maybe the poem wasn't great. Not as good as what Wordsworth and all those other fellows wrote. But I'm younger than they were. Maybe when they were my age they were only capable of writing nursery rhymes. It takes time to improve as a writer. You have to know about life, experience it. I'd experienced plenty on the Underground – enough to write about.

So too had the rest of the lads. As well as his football gear going missing, Mad Victor had six giant-sized lollipops robbed from his pockets. There was that much robbery on the Underground we didn't know where it was coming from. It was like going through the jungle and there were all these pygmies waiting to jump out and waylay us. At least, that's the way we felt.

After such a bad experience I did well to write a poem – any kind of poem. The only kind of writing most people would have bothered with would be a letter of complaint to whoever was in charge of the Underground. But I'm more able than that. Me – I wrote a poem that was a bit deep: intellectual. One that Mad Victor wouldn't understand. He doesn't know what a poem is.

I'd only just finished the poem when someone knocked on the door. It was Chippy. He was down in the dumps.

'What's wrong, Chippy?'

'Mr Glynn showed me a letter he got from the League the other day. I'm up before them Monday night.'

'Why the sad mouth? Ye knew it was goin' to happen. So what?'

'Well, me an' Mr Glynn, had a good chat. He said to be prepared for the worst, meanin' I could lose me place on the Dublin Schoolboys team. He says Little Hitler could be pushin' for it. Only I know there's no "could" about it. He'll be gunnin' for me, that's for sure, especially after the load of abuse we gave him on the phone yesterday.'

'There's more than Little Hitler on the committee. They're not all goin' to go against you. Anyway, you didn't do a whole lot, only chase a skinhead around the place. Nobody likes skinheads. They'll understand. Just tell them he was callin' Princess names, that you were only tryin' to sort him out.'

'There could be more to it than that. Remember the bits of gear I took from trainin'? They might try an' come after me for that, an' other bits of messin'. I've got a bit of a record with the League.'

'Forget it. Anyway, Mr Glynn is a good talker. He'll get you off. They'll listen to Mr Glynn. He's deadly in front of committees. Any time there's been trouble before he's always got us off.'

'There's always a first time for things to go wrong. In a way, it's overdue.'

'Don't worry, Chippy. You'll be all right.'

Chippy said nothing, just shrugged his shoulders. I knew by the look of him that he was sorry for every bit of messing he'd ever done while away playing with the Dublin Schoolboys. Maybe he was even sorry for all the messing he'd got up to with us. All of a sudden Chippy was a changed person. He'd be quiet as a mouse for the rest of the trip, at least. Maybe, in a few weeks, he'd come back to himself. When all the hullabaloo with the Dublin Schoolboys would die down. But for the moment, Chippy was one worried fellow.

Next day, we were all up bright and early for breakfast. There wasn't a sign of Harry Hennessy. One of the lads went to his room and knocked on the door. There was no answer.

'Harry's not in his room.'

'What do you mean?'

'I knocked. There was no reply.'

'You mustn't have knocked hard enough,' answered Mr Glynn. 'I'll go up. It won't take me long to get him out of bed. He's probably overslept.'

'Probably after all the beer he's had last night,' sniggered Growler Hughes. 'He's probably had a right skinful.'

Mr Glynn glared at Growler but said nothing. He didn't like us talking about Harry, especially about his drinking habits. He went up to Harry's room, knocked on the door as hard as he could. Then he turned the door-knob, but it was locked. He even tried shouting through the keyhole. Fearing the worst, he went down to the lobby and got the porter to come up and unlock the door. But there was no sign of Harry, the bed hadn't been slept in. He hadn't come home.

'Wha' are we goin' to do about Harry, Mr Glynn?'

'Don't know. Maybe he'll show up by the time breakfast is over. If not, we'll just have to go off without him.'

'Does that mean our trip to Wembley is off?'

'Sorry, but it was never on. Harry forgot to confirm it. I was just on to the crowd that runs the tours of the stadium. They didn't know what I was talking about.'

We didn't feel too good about not going to Wembley. Harry had let us down once again.

As disappointed as we were over there being no trip to Wembley Stadium we were really worried that something bad might have happened to Harry. Mad Victor wanted to ring the hospitals. There was always the chance he'd taken a heart attack and died, especially since he had been slugging duty-free whiskey all the way to London on the train.

'We might be goin' home with more than a few souvenirs in our bags.'

'Wha' ye mean, Growler?'

'We could be goin' home with Harry Hennessy in a coffin.'

'Don't be talkin' like that, Growler, He probably got drunk, fell asleep, and hasn't woken up yet. He'll show up soon as he comes to.'

But Harry hadn't shown up by dinner hour. We'd been out sightseeing most of the morning. We'd been to the Tower of London and a creepy place called London Dungeons. There were all these real-life dummies getting tortured – and rats. There were plenty of tourists there.

Mad Henry scared the life out of them in his leprechaun gear. He had brought a flashlight with him, thinking we'd be on the Underground again – so if the train broke down he'd be able to put it to good use in the tunnels. But he got plenty of use for it in the Dungeons. He bolted into the darkest corners and shone it from underneath his chin. What with his leprechaun suit and the sinister glow of the torch on his face, he scared the living daylights out of most of the tourists.

Only, this oul' lad caught him and gave him a dig. That caused blue murder with Mad Victor and we all got thrown out, all except Mr. Glynn. We'd only been in there ten minutes, so it was only right Mr Glynn tried to get our money back. But the man wouldn't give him a refund, said it wasn't his fault that we were a crowd of messers. What was worse, he said, some of the rats on show had gone missing, that we probably took them.

That was choice. Where were we to put them? In our pockets? Not likely.

12 Anyone for Rugger?

After dinner (it was a snack, but some of the lads kept calling it dinner) we went to a nearby park to play a match. Some of us wanted to go and see Arsenal but Mr Glynn said we'd have to turn up for the match Harry Hennessy had arranged against a local schoolboy team.

When we got to the park we had trouble finding the pitch. Only it wasn't a soccer pitch, it was something else.

'Them posts, wha' are they? Gaelic posts?'

'Rugby posts... I think...'

'You sure?'

'No. But they're not Gaelic posts, the cross bar is too high. Maybe they're for rugby... maybe they're somethin' else.'

None of us knew the first thing about rugby. We'd never been anywhere near a rugby pitch in our lives.

We weren't long in finding out what class of posts they were.

A lanky lad came out of the pavilion with a rugby ball. We were dead certain it was a rugby ball, because we'd found one once, only Mad Victor thought it was an Easter egg. That's until he tried to eat it.

'Mr Glynn, we're at the wrong pitch. Look, the soccer pitches are over there.'

And so they were. We could see them as plain as could be.

When the lanky lad saw us he went back into the pavilion. This oul' lad came out and began to talk to Mr Glynn.

'You the fellows from Ireland?' he asked.

'Yes, I think so...'

'Good. At least you sound Irish. All ready for the match?'

'We're all ready, only... is this a rugby pitch?'

'Why, of course. What's the problem?'

'We're not a rugby team. We're a soccer team.'

'A soccer team?'

'Yes.'

'I don't know where the mix-up could be. I

arranged the game with a Mr Hennessy when I was over in Ireland six weeks ago for the rugby international. I distinctly arranged a rugby match, with the emphasis on rugby. Is Mr Hennessy with you?'

'No.'

'Where is he?'

'We don't know. Maybe he'll show up later.'

'All this is very embarrassing. I don't know how such a mix-up could have occurred.'

But we knew how the mix-up occurred. Harry was probably plastered drunk at the time, and had got muddled. He doesn't find it hard to get muddled, especially when he's in the company of Arthur Guinness.

'Tell you what we'll do,' said the man in charge of the rugby team. 'We'll play one half rugby, the other half soccer. My lads are hopeless at soccer, you'll beat them flying.'

What he forgot to tell us was they were probably world-beaters at rugby. They'd trounce us. He was a real rugby type. Santa Claus whiskers and a striped rugby-club tie.

'Get togged out. I'll give you a quick run-through the positions and basic rules of rugby.'

'Don't bother, mister. We'd only get flattened.'

'No, you won't. It's easy, once you know how.'

About then the other team came out of the pavilion. They were kitted out in rugby gear: sweat-bands, scrum-caps, that kind of carry-on. They were much bigger than we were. They had a good look at us. We had a good look at them. We definitely didn't want to play

them in any rugby match. Anyway, we didn't know how to play.

And that wasn't all. Rugby being a fifteen-a-side game, on account of losing some of our gear down the Underground, we hadn't enough jerseys, boots and the likes to go around.

But we weren't going to tell them that, so we decided to act dumb and bluff our way out of the situation.

'We'll play the soccer first,' suggested Chippy chirply.

'That's all right, once we get some rugger in afterwards.'

And it *was* all right. We won 6-1.

With the soccer match over yer man was all set to get the rugby match going. Only, we weren't. We took off, still in our football gear, our clothes stuffed into our bags. We left Mr Glynn to do the explaining. As for us, we were gone, as fast as our legs could carry us.

Mr Glynn wasn't long in catching up. We put our clothes on at the side of the road and, eventually, made our way back to the hotel.

Harry Hennessy had returned. He was waiting in the lobby.

'Where were you, Harry? That was some match ye fixed us up with.'

'I got arrested durin' the night for singin' rebel songs at Marble Arch. I was put in a police cell. They only let me out an hour ago. Gave me a lovely fry for breakfast. They couldn't a been nicer. Real gentlemen. I wouldn't mind goin' back, only they probably wouldn't be as nice the next time.'

'Neither will we, especially after that rugby match ye fixed us up with.'

'What rugby match?'

'The one we're just after comin' back from. We only got out in time. We coulda got mauled to death.'

Harry wasn't impressed. He said he was going up to his room to get ready to go out for the night. Only, Mr Glynn wouldn't let him go out. He told him to stay in and watch the telly, along with the rest of us.

'Watch telly?' questioned Mad Victor. 'What d'ye mean?'

'No one's going out, especially when you can't behave. Anyway, the Eurovision Song Contest is on. It's worth watching.'

None of us thought the Eurovision was worth watching. But just to keep Mr Glynn happy we put up with his suggestion. To do away with the boring aspect of the Eurovision we ran a £1-a-head sweep on the outcome.

Flintstone won the pot. He couldn't believe his luck. He wanted to go out and spend the money as quickly as he could, only there was nowhere open, not at eleven o'clock at night. Other than that, he did three quick headcounts to make sure we'd all paid into the sweep.

Flintstone is daft, but not when it comes to money.

Some of us got the tail-end of 'Match of the Day' in the hotel lounge. Gavin Byrne was playing. With luck, we'd meet him the next day in Battersea Park.

13 Going Home

The match on Sunday morning in Battersea Park went without a hitch. We expected something to go wrong, but everything went perfectly. We even won. The only drawback was we knew our cup game back in Dublin against Lourdes Celtic was fixed for the same time. We didn't feel too good over that. We couldn't help but think of what was going on in Dublin. There would be Lourdes Celtic, after filling in the referee's card, lining up to centre the ball against absent opposition. Then the referee would blow the whistle, call proceedings to a halt, tell Lourdes to go home, and send the referee's card off to Little Hitler, who'd promptly award Lourdes a walk-over. We were out of the Dublin Cup.

Gavin Byrne showed up at the match in Battersea Park. We didn't half fall over one another trying to impress him with our football skills. We didn't bother passing the ball a lot. Instead, we made plenty of selfish individual runs, holding on to the ball as long as we could so as Gavin could see the various skills we had. The only one who sprayed the ball about was Chippy. I think he was fed up showing off his soccer skills over the last few months, especially with Little Hitler about to come down on him like a ton of bricks.

When the match was over a minibus parked in front of the pavilion. What we didn't know, not until we changed and came out of the pavilion, was that Gavin had organised the minibus to take us off for the afternoon for a feed and a tour of London Albion, his club's ground. We didn't think we'd get into a club ground on a Sunday afternoon, but there was no problem. The ground staff was doing some overtime, and Gavin had okayed everything with the club. We even passed Arsenal's pitch on the way. The coach halted for a few minutes but we couldn't see in, the walls were too high. Either way we were delighted to have the use of the minibus. Up until then we had to walk everywhere; either that or hang around for buses or use the Underground. It was sheer luxury having the minibus. Gavin Byrne was one real nice fellow. He was that nice we didn't once mess all the time he was with us.

When we saw London Albion's pitch we were dumbfounded. We'd often seen it on telly, but we'd no idea the place was so big. Not only was it big but the stands looked real posh. There were even executive boxes and a swanky restaurant. Not that we got anything to eat – it was closed – but we managed a good look around the place.

The groundsmen let us out on the pitch to walk around. We got our photo taken with Gavin Byrne in front of one of the goals. Gavin said it was the better of the two goals for scoring in.

'No matter where the pitch,' he said, 'most goals are scored at a certain end.'

Gavin had other things to tell us too.

'Don't mess; look after yourselves. It took hard work and dedication for me to get this far. Watch the kind of company you keep.

Some day you could end up a professional footballer like me.'

We knew none of us, except maybe Chippy, would end up professional footballers. None of us were good enough, and never would be. We could try all we liked; we were going nowhere, not in a footballing sense, We'd be lucky if we were still playing football at twenty. But, maybe, Gavin Byrne's advice wasn't directed at us; maybe it was meant for Chippy. If so, he was listening. You could see a kind of yearning look in Chippy's eyes once we got into the stadium. You could sense he wanted someday to be part of what Gavin Byrne had become.

Maybe Gavin Byrne's words of advice would rub off on Chippy. If so, the trip to London would have been worthwhile.

Like Gavin Byrne said, 'You've got to be able to listen and take things in.'

Anything Gavin Byrne said was gospel. If it were Mr Glynn, or Harry Hennessy, we wouldn't have listened. But Gavin Byrne... he was different class.

By the time Gavin finished showing us around the stadium we'd become confirmed London Albion fans; that's all except Flintstone. He is a Boston Celtic fan, all because an uncle has been sending him parcels of Boston Celtic stuff from America since he was knee-high to a front doorstep. What Flintstone doesn't realise – Boston Celtic is a basketball team. As far as Flintstone is concerned they're the best soccer team in America; one of the best teams in the world, even better than Glasgow Celtic. We're only wasting our breathe telling him otherwise. If he ever goes to America and sees them play, he'll be in for a big shock.

Gavin stayed with us most of the afternoon. Being a Sunday, there wasn't too much traffic so we got to see a lot of central London. We were due to get the train from Euston later in the evening, then take the night crossing from Holyhead to Dun Laoghaire. We'd be back in Ireland by six-thirty Monday morning.

It was hard to accept that the trip we'd been looking forward to for months was almost over. We all thought we'd get to see Arsenal or the likes play, but we got to see no one, not even Leyton Orient. And all because Harry Hennessy had arranged a so-called soccer match on the Saturday afternoon near enough to the same time all the top Premiership clubs were playing.

Trust Harry to make a cock-up! To think that we were so near to some of London's Premiership club grounds and didn't get a chance to see them play, except to catch a glimpse of Gavin Byrne's London Albion on BBC's 'Match of the Day'.

We'd get a right ribbing from our school-mates if they ever found out what really happened on the Saturday. Imagine, being in London and not seeing a top-notch match.' So we made up a plan to tell our school pals we went to see Arsenal v Liverpool and that we got to meet the players afterwards. We even organised a few fake autographs to prove the point. Well, there was no point in talking about our trip to England if we didn't see a top-class match. And it wasn't our fault that we didn't get to see Wembley Stadium, so we faked that too. We would say we went to Wembley on the Saturday morning. We bought a few postcards in a shop that showed Wembley Stadium close up, and at a distance.

We knew what we'd tell our pals:

'That's it close up.'

'That's it at a distance.'

'It looks better at a distance.'

'Yeah?'

'Sure. The further you're away, the better it looks.'

And that was Wembley Stadium.

Pity it was a Sunday, there were no shops open. There were Sunday morning markets, but we'd missed them. We would have liked to have gone shopping to get some presents. But the presents would have to wait until we got to the duty-free on the way home.

Home?

It was time to go home.

Later that evening, Gavin Byrne sent a coach to the hotel to take us to Euston. That way we wouldn't get waylaid on the Underground. Before we knew it we were on the train for Holyhead, our trip to London over. We were too down in the dumps to mess.

When we got to Crewe, Harry Hennessy got a terrible thirst to have a cup of tea.

'I'm just gettin' off the train a second.'

'Wha' ye mean, Harry?'

'I'm dyin' for a strong cup of tea.'

'Ye don't have to get off the train. Go to the dinin'-car, you'll get one just as handy.'

'Not likely. I'm not drinkin' that muck. I'll get one in the station. The train always stays in Crewe a good few minutes. Anyway, I know a lad who works here. He used to come to Bray on holidays, that's until it didn't stop rainin' one summer. I never saw him since.'

Some of us watched Harry walk across the platform into an office where the railway staff dossed. That was the last we saw of him for a few days. The train pulled out of the station without him. We thought he might catch up on a later train before the ferry left Holyhead, but there was no later train. Not in time for the ferry we were on. He'd catch the daytime

sailing; that's if he wasn't planning to stay over in some pub in Crewe.

He caught a morning ferry all right. Having no train ticket or money, some of the Crewe railway workers dressed him up in a railway uniform and put him on a mail-train bound for Holyhead. He arrived back in Dun Laoghaire early in the afternoon with the tunic buttons wide open and his belly heaving at top notch. He got the Dart to Bray and a taxi to his house. He flopped straight into bed and didn't get up for two days. The first we knew of it was when Mad Victor told us he met Harry in the post-office and got all the low-down. The biggest laugh of all – Harry was posting off a parcel to England. And what was in the parcel? The railway uniform he'd got in Crewe.

The rest of us got home to Bray just as our pals were getting out of bed to get ready to go to school. We had school too, only we were too tired after being up all night travelling. We were like walking zombies, only fit to go to bed, Chippy included, and he'd need to be wide-awake owing to being up before the Dublin Schoolboys disciplinary committee later that evening. His hour of judgement had arrived.

We all felt for Chippy. We really wanted him to get off – even when we heard he'd sold our vegetable round the previous Thursday to some geezer in a white van.

'He wha'?'

'He sold off the vegetable round last Thursday for fifty quid. He said the loot'd come in handy for the trip to London.'

'Why didn't ye say so before now?'

'Don't forget, it was Thursday night. Ye were too busy gettin' ready for the trip. Yer man did great business though. I followed him around the estate. All the oul' wans loved him. Said he'd a great selection of fruit-'n'-veg. He gave some kids free lollipops. They can't wait for him to come back this week. Ye'll never get the round goin' again, not with yer man around. Not when he paid Chippy fifty quid.'

All of a sudden me and Flintstone didn't feel too fond of Chippy. We hoped something bad would happen him. Something he wouldn't feel too good about. Something like his nose growing eight inches longer, or his hair falling out. Something weird, that'd be just fine.

First thing me and Flintstone did, after we got the bad news that the vegetable round was gone, was to bring the wheelbarrow back to the building site Chippy had taken it from.

We placed it on top of a pile of sand.

As we left, we could hear the rain splatter off its battered shape.

At that moment we felt a lot more for the wheelbarrow than we did for Chippy.

There's an old saying: 'What goes around comes around.'

Things, in the form of Little Hitler and his posse of a committee, were 'coming around' rapidly for Chippy.

To think, he had sold Flintstone and me down the river.

We took one last look at the wheelbarrow and headed home.